PATCHES OF FALL

Matthew Cooper

"Noah Sinclair!"

Dara yells from across the college campus cafeteria. His booming voice echoes with an occasional nasal pitch upward. This occurs when Dara pronounces the "S" in Sinclair.

"Dara Delpy!"

Noah calls back and smiles. Laughing at his fellow sociology classmate.

"And who's that ya have sitten there next to yah! Sinc old boy!"

The girl seated beside Noah Sinclair interjects.

"You know who I am Dara!"

Dara replies.

"Aye, I know yar face, but the name, that there I can't remember!"

The blonde hair covered girl whispers to Noah. Her eyebrows are inflected.

"What is he doing, people are staring."

Noah answers with.

"Just play along, he is getting a little too into his studies."

Rue looks at Noah Sinclair. Then at Dara Delpy.

"ok... Arg It be me, Matey, Rue Baker, your humble undertaker!"

Exclaims the girl with a quick breath and a slow giggle. Dara erupts into laughter before throwing his briefcase upon the lunch table. The table quakes Rue's pencil from her note pad. Rue's eyes follow her pencil gather a roll to the end of Dara's side of the table. Dara mirrors Rue's reaction as both sets of eyes watch the pencil roll off the end of the table and fall to the ground. Dara quickly switches gears to being his usual polite self.

"I'm sorry, let me get that."

Dara bends down to obtain the chewed-up pencil of his sociology classmate. He shifts his eyes to get a better look at what must be proof of her midterm anxiety. Bite marks deface Rue's pencil.

"Did you do that to your pencil?"

Dara asks Rue with the pencil extended to her.

"Nope, actually I needed a pencil and I found this one on the floor. I am not worried about the germs on it because, well, first I wiped it with hand sanitizer and I use a gripper as you can see there. I don't even need to touch the pencil really. And why waste a perfectly good pencil. It writes fine. See?"

Rue turns over her note pad to reveal a sketching of a fluffy black dog with big triangular ears like a cat-rabbit would have, except they belong on the face of a cairn terrier.

Dara looks confused. He looks at Noah to get a hint at if she is being serious or just messing with him. Noah laughs.

"She is an environmental studies major".

Noah nudges Rue with his left arm.

"Rue is a conservative."

Rue raises her voice a bit in response.

"Yeah you mean to say a conservationist, also I am a moderate as if to say I am not political and I don't care."

Dara's attention is still on the drawing.

"Did you draw that?"

Dara asks.

"Yes, this is my Scoland Terrier, Patches. He is a Scottish

3

terrier mixed with a west highland terrier."

"Does he look like that in real life?"

"You are going to meet Patches tonight."

Rue takes out her smart phone and slides through her pictures. One after another of the same dog taken at different times of the day. A couple pictures where Patches is wearing a Halloween costume, one as a pirate, and one where he is dressed up like a hot dog, even dressed as Santa Claus in front of a decked-out Christmas tree. This among various other poses of naps and the recent twelve-year-old birthday cake photo. This one is showing Patches wearing a yellow cone polka dotted birthday hat sitting behind an enormous cake surrounded with Rue's family. In it her younger brother and even younger sister, mom and dad. Patches' ears perked up in that moment of canine bliss. Seated behind a pink wax number twelve.

"Well he sure is cute, I like the name Patches. Why did you choose it?"

Rue excitedly answers as if a response to that question was on the study guide for this conversation. Through her blonde hair surrounding her pale face Rue examines Dara closely.

"Do you really want to know?"

"Well, uh, yeah I do."

Dara comebacks but Rue goes over the top with.

"Oh so, you're mad?"

A serious look in the college Dara's direction. Sinc hears this and closes his textbook. Dara crunches his brow down.

"What? No? I mean I want to know why his name is Patches but you don't have to tell me."

A bead of sweat drips down Dara's pale face off of black brows from black hairs. Sinc is watching this suffering take place and is amused into sudden laughter. Sinc's bangs split down the middle of golden-brown hair and winter blue eyes. Eyes that look like the same species of human that carry those bright blue eyes that Rue belongs to. Rue herself starts to laugh.

"You are mad because you did not notice the patches of golden fur in the puppy photo right here!"

Rue lifts her phone inches from Dara's face. Upon the brilliantly black coat of fur on Patches. There are large oval shapes of golden fur wrapping his back in pattern-less patches. These ovals morphed together creating the look of one dog with parts of another dog's fur sewed in. Dara pulls back away from the girl's phone.

"That is weird looking wow".

Dara says, Rue smiles and pulls her phone back. Locks eyes with Sinc.

"He grew out of his puppy fur and has regular fur now".

Sinclair reaches for Dara's briefcase. Dara snaps his briefcase from the table. He laughs.

"Yeah it's here, let's go outside and talk business".

Patting his briefcase Dara leads Rue and Sinc out of the cafeteria exit to the parking lot. Dodging their way through other students carelessly stuck outward chairs nearly tripping Rue into a wall when she had to decide to kick a student's foot, or step on the backpack, or trip over the leg of the chair, or the wall. Something was going to trip up Rue today. She opted to step on the back pack. A gamble that paid off because there was nothing in the backpack but hardback textbooks. Evident by their flat and firm structure. A sound was not made upon the trampling of the backpack. It would not have been known to the owner of the books and bag if Rue had not announced herself.

"Excuse me."

Rue frowns genuinely. The girl looks angrily and annoyed at Rue. The owner of the books and bag huffed out a breath. Raised her eyebrows, and picked her bag up off of the floor.

"Sorry I was about to trip."

Rue explains to the indifferent girl.

"You are trippin!"

Yelled the student at Rue before Rue hurries to catch up with the boys.

Awaiting Rue outside is Dara and Sinc. Already in the smoking section.

"Rue got yelled at in the middle of the cafeteria."

Sinc whispers to Dara. He laughs. Rue joins the young men by the squared off smoking section. It consists primarily of a bench, a bush, and two outside cone ashtrays on each side to collect the cigarette butts. This of course was redundant. Standing bush side, of the bench, Dara pulls from his pocket a pen. He brings it to his lips and breathes a vapor. Upon his inhale, the bottom of the pen, lights up blue. The brighter it gets with the increased pull from the lungs. Brighter and then the light turns to purple. He passes the pen to Rue, who on Purple inhales deeply the vapor until the intense purple light turns to red. On red Rue hands the pen to Noah "Sinc" Sinclair, who slurps in the liquid through the vaporizer pen until the red light turns out. Nodding in unison.

"One. Two. Three."

They exhale at once. Letting a large cloud of vapor explode upon the gray sky of this October morning. Dara pulls from his briefcase the Ouija board. Sinc smiles rubbing his hands together.

"This is going to be sick!"

Rue puts her hand on the Ouija.

"Ok. I can feel it. My house tonight. We are not really going to do witchcraft."

"No."

Dara responds. Before Sinc interjects.

"It's more of a film documentary, or a no budget horror

film."

Rue looks sternly at Dara.

"I want it just as I planned it. My idea, my house, my way. We are not doing real witchcraft; it is mock witchcraft".

The wind blows through Rues hair and the parking lot near the smoking section. This created a cascading tornado of autumn leaves. The tree debris twist and spiral through the courtyard in the distance. From the court yard powerwalks another student with a clip board. This student is short and a bit pudgy. He has a thin black goatee and thinning curly black hair. He is also making a B-line toward Rue.

"Oh, great, what is this going to be?"

Rue Disposes.

The three class mates watch as the young man comes nearer. Wind in his eyes before a cloud-move invites the sun. He crisps his eyes to see them through the ray of sunlight that finds a way to peak out.

"Hey I am Alex Strong; I am taking a survey for my sociology class."

Rue, Dara, and Sinc share a laugh.

"Yeah, for Dr. Brunswick, yeah?

Says Dara.

"That's right"

Alex smiles.

"We just did something similar, something about asking us about our fear of, or lack thereof, snakes?"

Alex smiles again.

"That is basically it. On a scale of one to five, five being the most afraid of, or one being the least afraid of. How afraid of snakes are you?

"Rue, age twenty-four, female. 4."

"Dara, age twenty-six, male. 1."

Noah, age twenty-seven, male. 1."

Alex quickly tallies up the numbers and jots down the demographics of the interviewees.

"Thank you guys I appreciate it."

"Anytime! Alex, right?"

 Asks Rue.

"Alex Strong."

Says Sinc. Before Alex can turn away after a chuckle. Dara asks.

"What are you going to do for your break of social norms project?"

"Oh, I don't even have a group yet for the project, I really have no idea what it will be on. Why? What do you plan on having?"

Dara taps on his Ouija board poking out of his briefcase. Alex smiles and nods his head.

"Nice."

"We will show you when it's finished."

"We'll email you!"

Sinc yells out to the back of Alex as he disappears into the cafeteria doors. The doors close behind him. Sinc pauses and looks at Dara. Sinc bursts out laughing. Holding the vapor device next to his face. His eyes are wet from a combination of autumn air.

"Whatever is in this pen is insane."

"It's ninety percent. It's no joke."

Sinc is face-smacked from what he inhaled.

"Can I have another slurp of this?"

Dara nods. While Sinc proceeds to sweep in a slow and steady stream of air through the vaporizer pen. Small pockets of vape cloud exits through his nose. On a sharp inhale the creeping clouds recede back into the nostrils. Sinc chokes. He gags. He spits up a little bit on his lip. Not enough saliva to disturb Dara or even Rue. Sinc sniffles. He breathes in. His nostrils arch before a large whaling out.

"Ah-chu! Ah-chu! Ah-chu!"

During this succession of sneezes, Sinc shoots out a strand of white snot from his right nostril. It hangs just below his top lip.

"Dude, wipe that thing, what is that one of the worms?"

Dara laughs and grabs Rue by the waist before whispering in her ear.

"What time are we coming over tonight for our little séance?

Rue blushes.

"My parents are supposed to be out of town until tomorrow night. So, anytime."

"You have the supplies, right? The grateful dead tabs?"

Sinc asks Rue who by this time had explained to him that she could only get two tabs, one for her and one for Dara.

"You can have mine, I have one left over from last summer, should still be good."

Dara looks over to Rue.

"It'll be fine. It is real stuff like the grateful dead tabs. I did one them this summer while I was doing some soul searching and believe me, it was real and I stored it properly."

BECKON THE VOID

Dara Delpy rides his bicycle down the street to Rue's house. He has known of her through mutual friends for over a year but never became close to Rue despite living in the same neighborhood. They met a few times before hand at a party or, once at the hospital to support a mutual friend. It wasn't until they have sociology class together that the two would hit it off. Their friend Noah, or Sinc would befriend Rue long before Dara would. Sinc was a bit suspect of Dara's intentions with Rue. This might also be from Rue cluing an attraction for Dara to Sinc. While Sinc, uninterested in Rue, in a romantic way also wanted to ensure that he can keep his best friend.

Dara rides up through the forested neighborhood of the Pines. He needs to employ the use of a flashlight on his bicycle along with a flashing back light just to keep from being hassled from Pines police. For good reason too. It was black at night in the pines. It was pitch black and Dara needed a light to see a place where he had gone before. And he needed to be seen by the occasional car of the busy commuter home.

"Ride with the flow of traffic."

The voice echoes in Dara's ears behind headphones. He listens to techno when he studies and when he rides his bicycle places. Peddling forward upon an incline gravel hill. Over the bump of a thick side root of one of the famous pine trees. He peddles pass non-cookie cutter cottages. Each yard different than the last. Houses painted in the night color of a paler version of their daytime selves. Dara glides passed the pond aligned with several large maple trees and dozens of pine trees. The geese outnumber the trees. They honk and flap and float and waddle walk. They assume crossing the road at their leisure is a given. Most every car will stop for the line of crossing geese. The geese of the pines seem to have learned that behavior. Dara cuts through the break in the line of geese marching across his path to Rue's séance. Forward to Rue's house where he is to meet up with Sinc and Patches.

Dara peddles and cracks a sound to his ear. It was his knee. His right knee on the peddle downward up the second incline of the bike trip. The pain shot to his nerve yet he kept peddling forward. Knowing he is going to be feeling it later, nevertheless, he wants to accomplish the task of taking the bicycle instead of the truck to avoid driving while tripping on acid later. Dara becomes nervous and begins repeating a mantra.

"Whatever happens, it's going to be interesting, whatever happens, it's going to be interesting."

Dara repeats this to himself three times before drifting into Rues driveway. Patches is at the storm door barking wildly. Rue emerges from the darkened orange glow of the hallway after the entrance of her parents' house on the bay. Rue smiles waving Dara in. Just as that happens Sinc pulls in fast. Rues eyes get wide. Dara turns squinting eyes to Sinc's headlights. Brakes squeak and Sinc comes to a gravel halt inches away from hitting Dara.

"Nice."

"Hey, sorry man you came out of nowhere."

Sinc slams his door shut.

"Yeah I came out of nowhere? What were you doing flying

in here like that, kids play on this road!"

"Calm down Dara, I said I was sorry!"

"You just need to be more responsible Sinc!"

"Me be responsible? where's your blinking light thing for your bike?"

"Dude I just turned it off when I pulled up!"

Rue is watching the argument; she can be seen by Dara tapping her foot through the storm door. Sinc pleas with Dara.

"Dara, I am sorry I almost hit you, on your bike, with my car. I will be more responsible next time. Now, come on, can we, let's go do a college project while tripping on acid."

Dara laughs and walks inside greeted by the barking hair pile called Patches. Sinc follows. Breaking the ankle biter from Dara's pant leg.

"Hey Patches, Patches, little Patches shu-zu-zu-zu-shu, little buddy!"

Sinc embarrassingly lays upon the creature loads of affectionate petting and scratching. Patches lays on his back kicking his foot at the right scratch.

Rue breaks up the love fest.

"Patches, be a good boy and go lay down!"

Patches ears perk up. Little brown eyes locked on his master. Patches got up to his four feet. He wagged his tail before he ran upstairs to a bedroom. Rue watches with motherly pride.

"I am going to have to get him a treat."

Dara opens up a pill bottle. Rue notices, offering Dara a bottle of water.

"What pills are those?"

Sinc asks.

"It's a mood stabilizer my psychiatrist has me on for my bipolar mania. It's called Lamictal."

"What does it do?"

Rue asks handing a water to Dara. Upon receipt he opens it.

"Well it is supposed to calm me down and keep me mellow so that I don't flip out on someone or act weird as a symptom of my mental illness."

"Are you going to be good to trip well with us during the séance?"

Rue asks.

"You're not going to lose it on us are you man?"

Sinc asks.

"Yeah I have been on this for over a year sometimes I get a really bad rash from it. I have a steroid ointment for if and when I break out in what Is called, "Stephen Johnson's syndrome.""

"Stephen Johnson's syndrome?"

Asks Rue.

"Yes, it is a vicious hives rash that takes over the whole body in days or even hours. Sometimes leading to death. It's because when you are allergic to it, you are really allergic to it. Not me, but I do have a mean rash on my leg right now. Look!"

Dara pulls up his left pant leg to reveal two large lemon sized rashes on his pale leg oozing pink slime from being scratched raw.

"Dara that looks infected!"

Exclaims Rue.

"It's not, I am on antibiotics "

Sinc interrupts sarcastically.

"Well that is fascinating, are we here to talk about our crazy friend's rash or are we going to trip and do some cool witchcraft stuff!"

"Sinc, it is not witchcraft stuff, it is a mock séance. But yeah, I am excited let's do this."

Rue looks at Dara before leading him and Sinc upstairs to her room. The go to a room where Dara can see Patches glowing eyes from the room across the hall as the furball lies down. His nub of a tail wagging.

"Cute!"

Yells Sinc, spotting Patches.

They enter through a door and hanging beads into the hippie den that is Rue Baker's room. The tie-dye Bob Marley tapestries next to ones with Jimi Hendrix. The grateful dead bears make numerous appearances. Large peace signs, pot leaves, sunglasses and bongs. The floor was wooden and the ceiling fan overhead did not work. Rue pulls out a painting kit.

"What's that for?"

Dara asks Rue with a finger pointing at the zip lock bag of paintbrushes and acrylic paint.

"It's for our pentagram."

Rue says this while spraying down an area directly underneath the ceiling fan with all-purpose cleaner before wiping any dirt or dust away. Rue takes out the white paint and applies the paint directly to her floor in a large circle.

"You guys are going to help me clean this up before my parents get home, right?"

"You think now, after you got started is a good time to ask me for clean-up help? Yeah Sure."

"I'll help you Rue."

Dara says to the rolling eyes of Sinc.

Rue proceeds to paint a five-pointed star connecting the circle in the center. Each point, an equally placed spoke on the wheel. She pulls from her bag, black paint. She squirts out the paint on the floor.

"You know what we forgot to do you guys? We forgot to take the acid".

Rue Giggles and pulls out a plastic zip lock with two small pieces of paper in it. She pulls out one on the middle and one on the index finger. A picture of a bear. The grateful dead bear. On the grateful dead tabs. She places one bear tab on Sinc's tongue and one on her own. Dara pulls out what he had stashed. A blank small piece of white paper. He places is on his tongue. The trio sit with legs folded on the floor. Each end they sit an equal distance away. Dara paints with the brush in his left hand. Sinc his right, and Rue is also left-handed. The three work to complete a white, black, and red pentagram three feet in diameter. Rue stands upon a chair and looks down on it.

"It's almost done!"

Rue sits back on the ground and continues to paint for a few more minutes. Rue stands up on the chair again. She gazes down at the pentagram.

"Yup, it's almost perfect!"

Rue sits back down to paint more minutes added to the project. Dara and Sinc wait patiently. Having a sort of silent agreement to not say anything. What they might be thinking. That the pentagram is finished and Rue is taking too long to finish her final touches. But they do not say a word about it and wait and let Rue take her time. The girl creaks up on the chair looking down upon their pentagram. She smiles.

"It looks pro as shit."

Dara points up to the ceiling fan.

"Is that where we are putting the cell phone to record this. And a side note, does anyone feel it in their toes?"

"Dara, I have been feeling it for the past ten or so minutes."

"What about you Rue? Rue?"

Rue is sitting aside the pentagram with a giant smile plastered on her face. Her cheeks curl up and the back of her teeth can be seen. Her eyes are not matching the smile on her face. She looks frozen. Deadly frozen. She raises her right arm over her head. Her index finger crawls along the wall in search of the switch. She finds it. Rue turns out the light.

"Rue, what's wrong with you?"

Dara laughs nervously.

"What the hell is this!"

Sinc yells. Rue's eyes dart over to Sinc. She bats a lash at Dara, and starts to laugh.

"Yeah I feel it you guys!"

Rue turns the lights back on and fashions her cell phone to one of the fan blades. She hits the record button and rotates the blade to center over top of the location of the pentagram.

"There, perfect. We will set up and light the candles, but first..."

Rue leaps from the chair in the middle of her room to her bed. She scurries across the floor to her closet. Dips inside the dark room for a split second. Then emerges holding three matching black hooded robes and three matching white expressionless masks. Rue throws her mask on and lays on the floor on her back next to the painting of the pentagram. She crosses her legs and bounces her bare foot up and down to a beat in her head. Dara climbs up the chair and rotates the fan blade to him to check to see if it is still recording.

"Oh, you better be ready!"

Dara says as he sends the phone back to its previous position; via the fan blade rotation. The fan squeaks. Sinc is sitting out of camera focus putting on his robe and mask. The ray of light coming through Rue's window reflects off the china white masks. The three of them start to bust out laughing at the spooky sight of one another. Their voices changed deeper as the soundwaves channel through smaller chambers. Rue's tongue swabs the slim mouth hole when she speaks. The inside of the mask rests on the warm cheek. It did not take long for sweat to start to collect inside Dara's mask. Rue takes out another bag from her closet. This one has candles in it. She lays out thirteen single candles around equal distances from another. In the bag is two long red candles. Rue giggles and places a large red fourteenth candle in the middle of the pentagram. A match is struck in a dark room. The glow transfers from the match to the candle in Rues hand. She holds it to the long red candle in Dara's.

"Light, to each end!"

Two candles start in the center candle, lighting it. Rue and Dara split the candles on opposite ends. Each half are to be lit. One by one the succeeding candles are lit until all are glowing tall. Three white masks reflect orange stars from candles. Slowly Rue lifts from her lit end, she moves her candle to the awaiting unlit. Dara mirrors Rue. Passing his torch to the next unlit. Aflame. To the next. Aflame, meeting Rue in the middle Just in front of Sinc. There on the North end of the star left an unlit. One left. Sinc aggressively takes from Rue's hand the long red candle. He leans forward extending his arm to light the last candle. In his swiftness with Rue, however, he managed to put out the candle nearest to him. Dara signals his candle to show Sinc what he had done. Upon notice Sinc quickly hovered his candle over the unlit. Aflame. All the candles are lit.

Rue announces.

"Hey guys, you know what we forgot to do? We forgot to take out the mouse?"

Dara and Sinc laugh.

"Seriously you guys we forgot the mouse. Get the mouse, get the mouse."

Sinc sasses back.

"You, get the mouse, get the mouse".

"What mouse?"

Dara asks big pupils to the enlarged ones of Rue. A grin on her face cannot be seen behind her white mask.

"The sacrifice!"

Rue hops to her feet. She disrobes before lifting her mask from her face. Dara watches her frisbee it to her bed. Sinc looks at Dara who is flabbergasted.

"I guess, you want to go to a what? Pet store?"

"That's correct, we need a mouse to play our sacrifice in order to make our mock séance look more convincing."

Replies Rue to Dara. Sinc is blowing out candles one by one. Dara disrobes and Sinc follows suit. Rue leads them in the direction to the driveway. A phone rings.

"It's my sister."

Rue smiles at Dara.

"Hey, what's up?... You're going... Cool, well, be safe. Me? I am with Sinc and Dara from class working on our break from social norms project for sociology. We are doing a satanic movie!"

Rue laughs before sliding out of the call.

"What did your sister say?"

Sinc asks.

"She's going to a party and staying with her friend tonight."

Says Rue. The three arrive to the driveway.

"Sinc, you got me blocked in."

"I guess, Sinc, you're driving."

"No, I can't, I'll back out and let Rue drive her car".

Sinc looks at the black outline of his car. It is pitch-black. Yet the form is shifting subtly. Like a tiny wave perfectly spiraled down from the orange glow of Rue's house painting itself on Sinc's car.

"Can you just let Rue drive your car?"

"What? No, look at her, she is rolling face."

Rue is pumping out low giggles.

"I am rolling face."

She laughs.

"But I can drive. Sinc! Back out!"

Rue climbs into her white jeep. Dara makes his way to the passenger seat When he hears Sinc yell to him.

"I forgot my keys upstairs, Sorry!"

Sinc runs through the storm door passed the tail wagging of Patches, up the stairs to the right and first door on the left. He grabs his keys from Rue's dresser while simultaneously knocking over Dara's Lamictal bottle. The cap is loose that when the bottle hits the floor twenty-nine white circular tablets fall out near the opening. Sinc in a frantic, scoops them up in the bottle really fast. He looks on the wood floor to see if there are any stragglers. He doesn't see anything of left-over pills. He sees nothing except the lines in the floor as they start to wave at him. Sinc puts the cap on the Lamictal bottle tight and places it back on Rue's dresser before running outside.

"Peace Patches!"

Sinc whispers to the little beast before breaking through into darkness. Then Rues headlights blind him.

"Damn turn off your Brights!"

Through the rolled down window.

"Those are not my Brights! These are my Brights!"

Rue flips a gauge next to her steering wheel. Dara watches as steam starts to rise from Sinc as he stands, bathing in the high-beams.

"It burns!"

Sinc runs to his car to back out, and let Rue out. A quick maneuver and Sinc hops into the back seat of Rues jeep. Before leaving the Pines, Rue comes to a stop. It is for the geese of the Pines. Eight large Canadian geese waddle walk in a line across their path.

"We got to wait for these turkeys!"

About thirteen hatchlings follow the grown-up geese.

"Aw, I could have hit one those things. So tender, look Dara."

Rue says before she imagines a figure of a man. The man is waddle walking with the geese. He is naked and appears to be quite old. Rue shakes this thought away from her head and accounts it to be the workings of the grateful dead tab that is still dissolving on her tongue. The geese proceed on into the darkness of the pond. Rue drives on in the direction of the pet store.

STRYKER AND PEPPER, HORROR ACTORS

"I need a stiff one after that car ride!"

Sinc yells out upon walking into the pet shop. Rue and Dara slope-in wiping weary eyes. They refocus to see none other than Alex Strong behind the counter. Alex's eyes get big with surprise. He is wearing his blue apron and name tag ready to assist the customers.

"Oh, hey guys, how is the project going?"

The group look as if they had forgotten why they are there. Each pupil in their eyes is like its own planet.

"Yeah, the project."

Rue ques over to the rodent section visible from the main hallway. She walks past aisles with fish tanks and other aquaria. She walks past reptile terrariums, UVB lights, heat lamps, various substrates and vitamin feeding-accessories.

Standing by the counter in a daze, Sinc speaks to Alex the best he can.

"Mouse, get the mouse, we need a mouse for the Sacrifice."

Alex shrieks.

"What! A sacrifice?! Those mice are for pets or for feeding to snakes or hawks. You can't just tell me that you plan on killing this animal. Not just to kill it."

Dara hears this and puts in an effort to save the sale.

"No! No, we don't plan on killing the mouse! It will be a horror actor for our project. It is a no budget horror movie. Look!"

Dara points to an associate taking out a snake to show Rue.

"Wait, what is Rue doing?"

Dara looks over to Sinc. Sinc's face waves into a triangle and holds that shape. Sinc's head appears to turn into the top of a pyramid. It resembles that of a flounder. Or half-flounder, half-man.

"Dude is Rue buying a snake?"

Dara asks to the gills of his once familiar friend. What appears to be a new look for him. Dara whispers.

"This acid is crazy; you look like a trout or something. I swear, if Rue is buying a snake. She just said she is afraid of snakes earlier."

"Acid changes people."

Alex interjects. Dara and Sinc look at him.

"Whoops, cat's out of the bag now."

Alex looks at Dara with widened eyes.

"Can I get some Acid? I always wanted to try; I get off when we close in a few minutes."

"Yeah I don't see why not. Let me ask Rue if she has anymore, and we can hang out and do this project together."

Alex's eyes light up as if Dara answered his sacred prayers.

"That is awesome, I mean it helps me out too because I don't have a group yet anyway."

"Seriously though, is Rue buying a snake?"

Dara asks as Rue and an associate stumble up to the counter.

"One ball python and four adult male mice comes to ninety-three twenty-eight."

Sinc eyes well up. He connects with Dara who equally is stunned at Rue.

"What? We need supplies."

Alex turns pale red. Dara whispers to Rue while she pulls out her credit card.

"I am sorry, I invited Alex along with us, he is down to trip with us and gets off, like now."

Dara nods and his eyes meet that of Alex's.

"I hope you have more for him because the grateful-dead tabs were all that I had."

Rue explains. Dara looks at Alex with a shoulder shrug. Rue fills out the paperwork for buying the snake and what the pet store calls fancy mice. Sinc opens the mouse box. The fancy mice are more beautiful than the feeder mice that look like lab mice, all white. The ones that Rue bought are usually sold as pets because they have patterns on their fur. They look like mouse-hamsters. One in particular, the runt, had black fur on its back like a winter coat, fluffy and with brown fur sprinkled in.

"I like this one, let's call the little one Pepper."

Says Sinc. Rue finishes up the paper work and proceeds to the door. Dara follows motioning to Alex that it is time for him to go. Sinc follows carrying the mouse box.

"Dave I'm leaving, they are my ride."

Alex throws off his apron upon rolling it up under his arm. He powerwalks to catch up with the group.

"Nice you came, we don't have any more tabs but I have something for you."

"That's cool, I am just happy to get out of there and get this project finished. What the hell are you guys doing with all the Animals?"

Rue interrupts.

"My sister saw that I posted the picture of the mouse and told me not to kill it!"

Rue laughs swerving out of the parking lot.

Alex looks at Dara with a slanted brow.

"We are not going to kill the mouse. It is for the project. We are going to do a mock séance. Don't worry."

Dara explains to Alex. Sinc is quietly becoming himself again in the eyes of Dara.

"Are you guys still feeling it?"

"Feeling what."

Dara hears a voice in his head.

"Feeling what Dara? What are you feeling Dara?"

The voice in his head starts to scream.

"Dara! Feeling what! What are you feeling!"

Dara Screams.

"I feel like I am rolling face!"

The car erupts into laughter. Alex joins in the fun too as Rue swings her car into her driveway.

"I think I will have that drink now!"

Sinc yells to the empty house of Rue. Patches stretched out leaning on the storm door barking away at Alex.

"Hey Patches!"

Dara yells to the Scoland terrier, the half-Scottish, half-west highland whose ears perk up.

"The little mut is cute."

"Scoland right?"

Alex says to Rue.

"Yeah, how did you know? No one knows that breed."

"Scolands are such a popular mix in some circles, that is became its own breed. The Scoland."

"Yes! I know, they are the cutest dog, did you see my bumper sticker?"

"I heart my Scoland! Yeah!"

Alex laughs while walking into Rue's house. Alex dodges passed the barking Patches who is being distracted with scratches from Dara.

"Patches stomach is red as hell right now."

Rue hears this and walks over to her puppy to examine him closely.

"Oh, that, it's just a little rash, he gets those a little bit this time of year. C'mon let's go upstairs and set this séance up!"

Patches is left to his scratching. Dara walks up the stairs watching as Patches kicks his leg across his body ferociously. This only causes the itch on Dara's leg to become more noticeable to him. Dara bends down to run his fingernails over his clothed leg. He knows he should not scratch. The doctor made that much clear. But he needs to scratch. It feels too good to sooth that burning-itch of an eczema rash. He digs into the wound. He can hear the scab break. The scab that took days to make is broken down into an oozing uncomfortable and itchy wound. The moisture from the blood and inflammation seep through Dara's pant leg as he walks up the stairs to Rue's room. Patches can be heard gnawing at himself. The sound of which only temps Dara to scratch more. However, Dara escapes any further digging and proceeds into Rues Room through her decretive beads. He over hears Rue explaining to Alex what is going to be done.

"Dara pay attention. Someone is going to have to handle

the snake."

"Right, Dara and Sinc have a fear index 1 of snakes."

"Correct, so one of you guys has to hold the snake."

Rue hands the boxed animal to Dara. Dara obliges popping open the top.

"Wow she is a real beauty. Ball python, nice!"

The snake curled firmly around the bony pale wrist. It was black and gold with natural wavy-gridding that occurred around its sides. The underbelly was pale white. The python must have just shed because it was smooth as silk. Flicking its tongue, the tip of which is pink. The rest is black. The eyes of as ball-python are like two little black buttons non unlike the eyes of Patches. Upon closer inspection, the famous diamond-eyes of the snake can be seen within those blackish buttons.

"Why did you buy four mice? I get the snake, that is dope as hell, but why that many mice?"

Alex asks Rue who answers with...

"First one mouse seemed like enough but then I felt bad about taking the mouse away from his friends. I knew when I bought these animals that I was going to return them the next day. Sorry".

Rue frowns at Alex. Then she smiles.

"So, I decided to just buy all the male fancy mice in the cage. Then I can complete this project and the mice get to go to a sleep over somewhere cool."

Alex looks over and sees a two-foot glass bong sitting in the corner of the room.

"The pentagram looks dry!"

Cries out Sinc. Rubbing his hand over it.

Dara noticing the direction of Alex's gaze. The direction of the bong. Asks rue.

"Can we spark that thing up. Its dancing at me."

Rue walks over to her dresser. She steps over the penta-gram before pulling out a drawer. Rue pulls out as small black con-tainer. She pops open the lid and a smell of a skunk comes into the room.

"Wow I can smell that from here."

Says Alex from the other side of the room. The shorter of the group approaches Rue with the glass water pipe in hand.

"So there really isn't any more acid?"

Sinc laughs.

"There really is no more grateful-dead tabs and this tab is all I have."

Dara sticks his tongue out to show the little square piece of paper dissolving on it.

"You still have that on your tongue?"

Says Sinc.

"You can swallow that now"

Says Rue with a laugh. Dara Gulps it down.

"I am rolling-face you guys."

Dara says.

"It comes and goes doesn't it?"

Rue replies.

"This is so sick!"

Says Sinc.

"I kind of feel left out."

Alex says before taking a large inhale of the glass water bong. The bubbling can be gently heard as air passes the percola-tors. Alex coughs loudly causing the water in the bong to back fire out through the top. Erupting out is a mix of watery ash, steam, and smoke.

Rue, Dara, and Sinc laugh at the face that Alex makes. He is sorely red.

"I am so sorry."

"We are not stressed about it."

The three seem to say in unison. Rue darts to her bed to pick up her mask and robe. Signaling to the others that it is time to robe-up and put the mask on.

"Lights, camera, action!"

Alex sits on Rues Bed.

"I am so high right now!"

Alex says laughing red and squinting through heavy eye-lids.

Rue, Dara, and Sinc stand at equal distances from each other around the pentagram. Their cloaked capes drop against the painted floor. The candles in place.

"Alex, hit the lights!"

Rue with a candle in one hand along with Sinc. Dara holds the python. The python slithers up his arm. The cold scaly skin of the reptile gives Dara a chill down his back. The snake begins to slither into the cape, under the shirt. Dara quickly repositions the snake to a more manageable spot. Alex hits out the lights. The room goes black. Match strike and glow.

"To each end!"

Rue lights the glow of her candle from the middle candle to her side. Aflame. Sinc follows until every candle is lit. Aflame. Then the last candle North of the pentagram. Aflame.

"Every candle is lit. Now what?"

Asks Alex.

"The sacrifice!"

Hisses Rue. Three white glowing expressionless masks dart in Alex's-direction.

"Get the mouse, get the mouse!"

Rue's voice comes out deep and Sinc puts his candle out and walks slowly to the box with pepper the mouse in it. He plucks the little rodent from his three friends. Pepper squeaks out a sound that attracts Patches. The dog's scratching can be heard on the door. Then a faint canine moan of intrigued begging. Sinc walks toward the pentagram's center. He raises the rodent high to show to the recording phone camera overhead. Then he lowers Pepper unto the pentagram platform that is a wall of candle light. The mouse scurries around the pentagram between the candles. Room enough to easily walk about unpanicked. Alex watches in mesmerized-horror as Dara places the snake down onto the pentagram. The snake slides between the candles. The mouse walks up in the direction to the snake's head.

"Get the mouse!"

Cries out Rue as Alex stands up. The snake strikes. Pepper squeaks. Scratching can be heard on the door from Patches again. Pepper is coiled up by the python in a second. Before anyone can react the twitching leg of the mouse stops.

"Pepper is no more."

Says Sinc.

"That is irreplaceably messed up!"

Yells Alex in anger.

"You said you were going to return the animals? Alive!"

The room goes silent for a moment. Dara looks at Alex. Alex is hyperventilating.

"It was an accident; we did not mean for the snake to actually eat pepper. Look he is swallowing him now!"

Rue points to the snake who is standing tall like a cobra maneuvering his jaw to lower the mouse further down his throat.

The tail of the mouse is left hanging before slowly receding down the cold esophagus of the ball-python. Alex watches with morbid-fascination as within minutes the snake completely devours Pepper the mouse. Sinc decides.

"The snakes name should be Stryker."

The snake is left to digest the rodent modestly before Dara scoops Stryker back into his box.

A sound is heard from outside the door. It's the cries of Patches.

"Something is wrong with Patches."

Rue goes to investigate. She swings her door open in a fury, knocking off the strands of beads that dangle from it.

PATCHES SYNDROME

Rue looks to see. Patches is not there. Yet on the outside of the door lay blood marks. Paw prints made of blood.

"Patches is bleeding!"

Rue screams in horror. Seeing the threads of blood pull down about a foot from the bottom of her bedroom door.

Rue pans her gaze down the hallway in a quick search for her dog. No sight of Patches. The only thing she sees is what looks like a clump of fur the size of a fist. She walks over to it. Before she arrives at the stairwell, she bends over to pick up the clump. It is Patches' fur. It has been pulled from the hair follicles. A drop of blood can be seen. It is a clean drop on the end of the clump. The follicle that housed Patches shining black fur has been forcefully chewed, or pulled out, and a piece of the skin is still attached. Rues eyes water.

"Patches! Come here good-boy!"

No answer.

"Patches!"

Rue wails an outward cry. The stress in her voice is tightened.

"Patches!"

She hurries down the stairs walking passed another fist-sized clump.

"Patches must be hurt."

Dara follows Rue downstairs passing the clump of hair. Dara watches Rue slowly walk down the hallway towards the kitchen. Stepping by paw prints made of blood. Rue stops ahead of Dara. She gasps and flicks the light on. Dara meets with Rue at the mouth of the kitchen. There Sits Patches wagging his nub of a tail on the floor next to his leash. He is wet with blood. He starts scratching himself furiously. With each scratch, blood and skin are scraped away and sprayed onto the waste can next to him. Rue screams. The dog blood paints a pink mist on the veneer of the floor.

"Holy hell, what happened to Patches!?"

Sinc stumbles in and goes to the refrigerator to make himself a drink. Patches stops scratching and looks to Rue before letting out a cry. Rue grabs up Patches. Holding him to her chest and crying with him. Patches is getting blood on her sweatshirt. Patches has lemon sized rashes on his stomach. The sores are also around his face and neck oozing and bleeding from his scratching. He is wet from the amounts of ooze dripping out of his sores.

"Patches definitely needs to go to the hospital."

Says Alex.

"I know he is like; he is shaking. Let's go!"

Yells Rue, ready for action.

"I am just going to go home and try to sleep; I am having a bad trip now anyway. I am sorry about Patches but I should go."

Says Dara with sad eyes at the shaking mass of flesh that once resembled a family pet. Patches cries, Rue and Alex leave.

Dara follows them and the squealing dog outside. He sits on his bicycle.

"I am just going to go home too Rue. I will talk to you!"

Yells out Sinc, heading to his car. Rue and Alex screech out tires. They pull out of the gravel driveway and take off to the animal hospital.

Dara starts peddling home. He looks up to the night sky and sees a peaceful freedom in the stars. Dara peddles relaxed and loosely on his way home. He has nothing to worry about because his bike-light turned on and he knows his way home despite being under the influence of drugs. Looks up ahead. There is something in the road next to the bike path.

"What is it?"

Dara thinks to himself. There are several things. Dara rolls up closer. The outline of a shape is beginning to take form. It is dead birds. It is the carcasses of several geese thrown about the road. A mangled neck and even a goose trying to fly away. The poor goose wing is broken and futilely, it tries to escape what has happened. Dara rides up on this honking tragedy. Dara lifts up his bike wheel over top the head of the goose.

"I'm sorry."

Dara pushes his bike down with the maximum force at his avail. The goose honks one last time before it is put to rest. Dara thinks to himself that this goose massacre must be from Rue on her rush to the hospital.

"Hell, there is like ten of you."

Dara talking to the bodies of the geese who find the road, their stone cemetery. He looks at the one he just put out of its misery. Dara picks up the dead goose by the wings and brings it in for a close embrace.

"I can feel your death my brother."

Dara says before folding the wings over the head of the

goose, shielding the world from his popped open skull.

"Well, goodnight."

"HONK!"

A goose flies over head startling Dara.

"Sheesh!"

Dara hops back on his bike to ride home. His shoulders are completely arched. When he arrives back home to his step father Glenwood's house. He takes enough sleeping meds to counteract the acid. Dara climbs through the Dark house stumbling through his bedroom door. Dara falls to his bed and thinks about Patches. What if Patches ate one of his Lamictal pills and got a case of a canine version of Stephen Johnson's syndrome? What if it had been his fault? Dara thinks to himself.

"Did I drop any of my pills when I took them out at Rue's house earlier?"

Dara imagines the mangled-up goose on the road and what it had in common with Rue's sick dog. Just covered in bloody sores. Dara Falls asleep and begins to dream.

IS THAT ONE OF
THE WORMS?

A dull pain in the pit of his stomach, Dara, wondering where he is, stumbles into an arched threshold adjacent to another walkway. The sound of cheerful blathering echoes off the shadowy hotel convention room. Dara follows an orange glow to the bar. He sits down elevated higher by the bar stool. Dara slides his boney hand across the glass-smooth-bar-top. Behind the bar was a busy man with his back turned making drinks for the larger mass of people at the party on the other side of this island-shaped-bar. The presence of the group was only hinted at by the loudened and joyous laughter. They can also partially be seen through glass shelves. His view is mostly blocked by the various bottles and types of liquor. Dara pans his head back and forth to see an attractive blonde woman in a white sweatshirt with Greek letters on it in purple. Her faint image poking out through the gaps in the displayed liquors. His detection of this almost familiar face is interrupted when the pain in his stomach knocks a noticeable inner pinch. The pain was sharp and Dara's stomach made an audible noise. The laughter stopped. Through the bottles and the stretched out green faces, Dara makes out the image of an older black man who is wearing a red sweatshirt bearing the same Greek letters. The figure of the man beams attention in Dara's direction. The wavy figures through the bottles all face the source of the noise. The music went silent, as did the rest of the party. Their eyes freeze on the now crouched over Dara, groaning in pain, and holding his bloated stomach. Dara looks up noticing a party of people looking at him.

"Dara Delpy!"

Proclaims a voice from the right side of the room.

"I haven't seen you in a while!"

Grinned a short and pudgy man his age wearing a sweat-shirt that donned the same Greek letters as the party on the other side of the bar. Unfazed Dara thinks back to what the source of this stomachache could be. Accounting for the previous meals he ate. Unable to consider anything odd that could cause a food born illness. The music and conversational celebration start up again. By now the smiling man is approaching from the right. The man slaps Dara's back.

"Dara!"

Taking a closer look and pausing on the sunk in eyes and bulging cheek bones of his old college friend.

"You don't look so good man."

The sympathetic eye of the short man finally grasps Dara's attention. He decodes the blurry face to be that of his old class mate, Alex. Alex had a goatee, just as he did when they first met. He was a little heavier since Dara left school. Dara mumbles a response in spite of the stomach cramps.

"You look a little on the thick side since I remember. I also remember you taking all the credit for my hard work."

Spilled out Dara to the wide eyes of Alex who went silent for a breath. Alex looks around to make sure that no one from his party overheard Dara's insult. Seeing the conversation carrying on as natural, his grin reappeared.

"Let me buy you a beer man, let's bury the hatchet."

Dara nods. Unable to mask the pain in his intestines. He inhales in an attempt to fess up to the reason for his sloped appearance. Before Dara can voice a word, Alex exclaims...

"Yeah I am a bit heavier than in college, but that never stopped me from getting my girl pregnant."

Thinking about his stomach and not about his old friendemy from community college, who appears to be trying to elicit a congratulations from him. Noticing Dara's condition, Alex beckons the bartender over.

"What it'll be?"

Says Lady Bartender.

"Two 1700 pale ales!"

Alex shouts at the red vested woman who quickly grabs the brown long necks wrapped with a red 1700 logo. She pops the top off of one and puts it in front of Dara. Alex, who is seeming to try not to be overly ironic. Alex says.

"Yeah, we been drinking 1700, really nice stuff, tell your dad that."

Alex snorts and grabs his 1700 from the bar tender. Dara looks at Alex and forces out a thank you. Alex waves over the attractive blonde woman from the other side of the bar, the smile still on his face. Dara seeing the incoming social assault wants to leave but the pain in his stomach keeps him tied to the stool. She approaches. Dara takes a gulp of his 1700. The proud Alex puts one arm around her and gesturing with the other to Dara.

"Madeline, this is Dara. Dara, this goddess is my Madeline."

The blonde Madeline rolls her brown eyes with a complementing smile. She was at least two inches taller than her future baby's father, but shorter than the average woman. Madeline extends her hand to Dara. Dara is breathing laboriously. He can feel a bead of sweat drop from a black strand of bangs to a crawl down his face collecting more and more of the minimal sweat droplets. The bead growing with each passing droplet that rests on the pores of the stomach ache stricken Dara. He raises his clammy hand to clasp Madeline's.

"Nice to meet you."

The girl's smile slowly faded. She looked away from the ghostly man that she just met. She looks to Alex. His eyes widened as he takes an exhausted breath.

"So, I have to ask what you are doing here, no offense man, but you never graduated!"

Madeline elbows her boyfriend's arm while nonchalantly wiping her hand off on her white-club-sweater.

Still fazed only by the cramps in his intestines, Dara takes a gulp of his beer. He wipes the sweat from his forehead and gives Alex a flat, and expressionless look. A smile curls on his face before the sickened clam-man glugs down what is left. Finished, he slams the bottle down on the bar top. Alex and Madeline's eyes meet. The two share an awkward yet hearty laugh. Madeline is clearly uncomfortable.

"Do you want another one?"

Asked Alex laughing at Dara, who is feeling better from the rare drink and is enticed to accept another. The Lady Bartender finishes mixing up a drink for Madeline. She Places a napkin down in front of the awaiting party-member.

"One Cat- Kamikaze."

The Lady Bartender gently pours the pale white liquid in a cocktail glass before Madeline. Dara puts his hand in a fist and rests it under his chin turning to the Lady Bartender. His eyebrows lowered.

"Cat-Kamikaze?"

Lady Bartender answered with.

"One-part vodka, one-part lime juice, one-part Triple sec, and whatever she is putting in it now."

The sharp long finger nail pointing at Madeline, who has dispensed the fillings of a half-red, half-blue capsule into her drink. Alex rolls his brown eyes this time with a look of disappointed surprise that appeared to Dara to be fabricated.

Dara raises the brew only to denounce the bully.

"Imposter!"

Pointing at the man's nose an inch away from touching it. Dara turns to address Lady Bartender wearing a red vest. She had short slicked-backed hair and her wrinkles seemed to lead to strands of gray.

"Don't accept this man's credit card! It's fools, it's all fools!"

Spat out Dara. He glugs down the rest of his second brew.

"Two more!"

He exclaims with a clenched fist thrown upon the bar top. Like a mad man his piercing eyes dart into the old lady. His green eyes yellow as he swipes the beer intended for Alex. In a shuddering movement the weakening Dara begins to feel the ache once again in his bowel's recesses. A headache becomes present from the social suffering, and all of this during the middle of what is supposed to be a routine beer delivery for Glenwood. He puts one hand on his stomach, his lips are pulling tight and with a heaving shout Dara demands Lady Bartender with a raised 1700 in the other.

"And prepare for me a Cat-Kamikaze!"

The ladies puff out a forced laugh.

"Looking white as Death. He must be serious."

Madeline obliges; pulling another capsule from her purse that she had looped around the back of her stool which is dangling too close to the floor. This prompted Madeline to perform some type of domestic acrobatics to acquire the ingredient. Madeline contorted herself, the sight of which amused Dara. Alex turns red. The stiff grin on his face disagrees with his eyes.

His eyebrows tilted mostly upward in the middle. Dara watches Madeline lean over the bar. She snatches a straw from a golden bar-caddy knocking it to the bartender's side of the floor. She laughs and proceeds to mix in the powdery white contents of the capsule before placing it directly into Dara's hands. He holds the cocktail glass up to his left eye and inspects Madeline's thumb print before he lowers the glass to his nose. Dara takes a four-second-long smell of the cloudy white liquid. He consumes the potion in one swig.

Alex looks over at the other side of the bar. The party is moving. He glances at his phone before he shoves it back in his hoodie pocket. He looks at Madeline. She is slouched backward looking past the stained-glass chandelier. The green polygonal abstract painted on the ceiling in emerald light captured her eye. Sixty-four large emerald trapezoids between one hundred and ninety-two diamond triangles.

"Let's go!"

Alex gestures over to the last of his peers filing into the banquet hall. He looks at pale Dara.

"You too!"

Alex grabs Dara by the hood, clenched like a dress sock. He pulses forward with a couple tugs. Dara takes his hood from Alex's hand.

"Ok, just don't do that, and don't act all aggressively."

Dara and Madeline follow Alex while he enters a grand white room filled with silver trays that display all kinds of food, sides, condiments, a salad bar, roast cutting board, and even a sushi bar. There were at least thirty circular tables that can each sit eight people.

"My bad, Dara. Look man, it's free food."

"I am anything, except hungry."

Dara scoffs at the food. Madeline laughs.

"Let me look at your eyes Dara."

Madeline requests with a forward approach. Dara can take a good look into Madeline's eyes for the first time. The light shines off of her enlarge pupils.

"Wow, are mine like that too?"

Madeline asks Dara, while gazing into bloodshot red rivers. His pupils were flush with his cornea giving him the appearance of having black eyes.

"Your eyes are really white and your pupils are huge."

"Well yours's are red, really red. Are you feeling ok?"

Madeline asks, before cutting off Dara's response.

"Alex look! It's Professor Thomas!"

Madeline slaps her boyfriend's back and grinningly waves to the white-haired woman with the same Greek letters thrown upon her sweatshirt. The woman makes eye contact with Dara. Dara watches her smile fade from her wrinkled face. Alex takes Madeline over to talk to professor Thomas. Dara leans back in his chair. He begins to feel a rush of euphoria from his cat-kami-kaze. The pain in his stomach seems to fade. The new annoying symptom comes from an itch, a little scratch in his throat. This did not bother him at the stomachache level from earlier. Still, it passed and Dara can feel more confident in what he is doing. Dara glimpsed the large movie screen. It is projecting a slide show of images. There is an image that catches Dara's eye. Among the photos from the club's activities from the year prior include one of Dara while he was in the club. Dara looks at Alex confused. Wondering why they would include a picture of him after being essentially banned. Alex is across the room with Madeline and professor Thomas looking at Dara and talking quickly within the group. Dara sits put where he is. He feels the scratch in his throat. He grunts out a wet cough. On the big screen it is a picture of Dara holding up sushi at his last banquet during his membership. It was orange and white striped salmon nigiri between the sticks with wasabi. Just like the same within the variety available to-night. A young girl with a microphone begins announcing names for awards as the slideshow transforms into a live feed via a video camera. The woman with the camera is following her around to different tables. Alex and Madeline come back to the table. Dara feels the itch in his throat. He belches. The couple sit down next to Dara. Alex explains to his weary associate.

"Thomas is not going to make a big deal about you being here. I told her I invited you. She just wants you to behave yourself, ya know?"

Over the speakers a women's voice announced the winner of the "Leadership award". "Madeline Fitzkerelli!"

Madeline stands up and the two older club members walk to her. One presents Madeline with a pin and a plaque. The camera lady captures the handshake. The live feed is broadcasted to the big screen and greeted with applause. A sickly Dara is captured by the camera. He appears on the bottom right of the big screen looking pale and about to be drenched in sweat. Dara feels the scratch again. The one in his throat. It's back. He coughs loudly. Dara is now center screen as a thin white string that he coughs up, rolls out from his tongue.

Alex yells and points at the white string hanging 7 inches out of Dara's mouth.

"What the hell is that?!"

Dara's eyes are agape. He is looking at Alex with sweat dripping down from his forehead. The message Dara sends to the old rival is one seeking help. It is in his eyes. The parasitic discharge is being broadcasted to the big screen. Among the shrieks and wales a woman can be heard speaking nervously.

"Was it the sushi? Did you eat the sushi? I didn't have any last year. Yeah, well, no. I had a piece last year. Oh God! It was only one piece. I am fine. I'm sure I'm fine, it was just one piece. Oh God!
"

One scholar sticks her fingers down her throat to induce vomiting. A few people are crying. Screams can be heard echoing off of the walls. Security guards pile into the room of people throwing up to a pale man pulling out his tapeworm. Dara grips the slimy worm hand over hand. Pulling the parasite out inch by inch. Alex sees this and begins screaming. Out of sheer mortal humility Alex gives Dara a hand at it. Alex's face is redder than ever with tears in his eyes as he pulls, aiding out the worm inch by inch. Little by little the elastic worm stops coming out. Alex pulls on it harder. Dara grunts in pain lisping through the worm.

"Dude easy, it's anchored to something in my stomach.

Alex pulls more gently. With the added tension spikes emerge from nature's rivets in the worm.

"It's spikey, Oh my god, its cutting into my hand. It hurts! It has freaky spikes coming out of it!"

Madeline runs out in a stampede of other club members. Crying, she abandons her half-eaten plate of sushi.

"Cut the feed!"

The picture of Dara looking healthy last year gets plastered on to the screen. With a big piece of raw fish. Then the slide show continues to another photo of new members at a zoo from the previous year.

"Cut the feed? Cut the worm!"

Dara yelps.

"Scissors! Please!"

Alex yells to anyone left in the room. Answered by Professor Thomas who wipes off chunky throw up from her face. She snatches a roll of silverware from the table. Then takes the knife. She sticks the knife into Dara's mouth. Coming close to cutting him. Thomas loops the six-foot worm around her steak knife. She goes the furthest within Dara's mouth as possible. She pinches the worm around the knife, severing the spiny white stomach dweller in two. One half of the worm recedes back into Dara's esophagus. The other half lay curled up on the clothed table.

"Dara Delpy! So, that is what's gotten into you?"

Announced his old mentor, Professor Thomas, pointing at a plate of uncooked fish. Dara Delpy panning the setting of tables littered with empty and partially drank 1700s. Rejects what he heard the woman say passively. He shakes his head.

"No. It was the 1700. It was Trisha Howe. My mother, the witch."

The older black man that Dara spotted from the other side of the bar over hears this as he did not abandon Dara either. He walks over with a 1700 in his hand. He sits next to Dara before confessing.

"If we all going to have a tape worm from drinking this 1700 then forgive me for saying that your mother is one, messed up, witch. "

Dara looks at him. The old club member holds up his 1700. He gives it a twist to reveal the floating spherical egg sac rolling along the inside of the bottle.

To be continued...

Made in the USA
Columbia, SC
14 August 2020

15242078R00029